FIELD TRIP DAY

ILLUSTRATED BY
Thor Wickstrom

BY
Lynn Plourde

Dutton Children's Books

An imprint of Penguin Group (USA) Inc.

JP
PLO

With love to my nephew Matthew, the wanderer

—L.P.

To Linda Pratt, gratefully,

—T.W.

DUTTON CHILDREN'S BOOKS   A division of Penguin Young Readers Group
Published by the Penguin Group • Penguin Group (USA) Inc., 375 Hudson Street, New York,
New York 10014, U.S.A. • Penguin Group (Canada), 90 Eglinton Avenue East, Suite 700, Toronto, Ontario M4P
2Y3, Canada (a division of Pearson Penguin Canada Inc.) • Penguin Books Ltd, 80 Strand, London WC2R
ORL, England • Penguin Ireland, 25 St Stephen's Green, Dublin 2, Ireland (a division of Penguin Books Ltd)
• Penguin Group (Australia), 250 Camberwell Road, Camberwell, Victoria 3124, Australia (a division of
Pearson Australia Group Pty Ltd) • Penguin Books India Pvt Ltd, 11 Community Centre, Panchsheel Park, New
Delhi – 110 017, India • Penguin Group (NZ), 67 Apollo Drive, Rosedale, North Shore 0632, New Zealand (a
division of Pearson New Zealand Ltd) • Penguin Books (South Africa) (Pty) Ltd,
24 Sturdee Avenue, Rosebank, Johannesburg 2196, South Africa • Penguin Books Ltd,
Registered Offices: 80 Strand, London WC2R ORL, England

Plourde, Lynn.
Field trip day / by Lynn Plourde ; [illustrations by Thor Wickstrom].—1st ed.
     p. cm.
   Summary: Juan Dore-Nomad, a boy who has a tendency to wander, provokes
mayhem on a field trip to the farm.
   ISBN 978-0-525-47994-9
   [1. School field trips—Fiction. 2. Farms—Fiction.] I. Wickstrom,
Thor, ill. II. Title.
   PZ7.P724Fi 2010
   [E]—dc22   2009022941

Published in the United States by Dutton Children's Books,
a division of Penguin Young Readers Group
345 Hudson Street, New York, New York 10014
www.penguin.com/youngreaders

Designed by Irene Vandervoort
Manufactured in China   First Edition

10 9 8 7 6 5 4 3 2 1

It was Field Trip Day.

Everyone in Mrs. Shepherd's class was anxious to visit a farm, especially . . .

Juan Dore-Nomad.

Juan knew that some of his best learning didn't always happen at school but during adventures out in the *real* world.

As the bus pulled out of the school parking lot, Mrs. Shepherd reminded the class about the rules.

"We know," said the students.

"Be polite."

"Stay with the chaperones."

"And keep your nose out of things."

"That's right," agreed Mrs. Shepherd. "And pay attention so you can see how a farm works."

When the bus pulled up to the farm, Mrs. Shepherd reminded the chaperones about their rules.

"We know," said the parents.

"No losing any students."

"Keep track of all *twenty-three* of them."

"Let you know right away if anyone is missing."

"That's right," agreed Mrs. Shepherd. "But make sure they have some fun, too."

Fandangle's Farm

The chaperones started making tally marks on their clip-boards. "We counted two sets of eleven, which makes . . ."

"Twenty-two!" shouted the students.

"Good math," said Mrs. Shepherd, "but wrong number. We're missing someone already. Everyone, look around."

Dewey noticed a pair of legs underneath a sign. "I found him!"

"Found who?" asked Juan as he peeked out.

"Found you. You're missing," said Dewey.

"No, I'm right here. Did you see this sign? It says 'Fandangle's Organic, Environmentally Friendly Farm.' I wonder what that all means."

"Well, Juan, let's go ask the person who knows," said Mrs. Shepherd.

Farmer Fandangle greeted them, "Welcome, everyone!"

"Mr. Farmer, what does your sign mean?" asked Juan.

"Oh, you'll see soon enough," said the farmer. "Let's start with the cows. But first, everyone, put these on." He held up booties and hairnets. "We can't have germs bein' spread."

"What can we catch from cows? Colds?" asked Juan.

"I'm not worried about *you* catchin' anythin' from the cows," answered Farmer Fandangle. "I'm worried about the cows catchin' germs from *you!*"

"Ya see, my cows give organic milk. I do everythin' I can to keep them and their milk natural and germ-free."

Farmer Fandangle demonstrated the sterile milking machines and milk vats.

Mrs. Shepherd said, "Milking sure has changed over the years."

"Yes, ma'am," agreed Farmer Fandangle. "Changed in a good way. Come on, let's head over to the henhouse next."

"Just a minute," said Mrs. Shepherd. "Before we go, time for a . . ."

"Head count," finished the chaperones. "We counted two sets of ten and had two extra students, so that makes . . ."

"Twenty-two!" shouted the students.

"Good math," said Mrs. Shepherd, "but wrong number. We're missing someone again. Everyone, let's get looking."

Drew heard a tiny rustling sound from a backroom in the barn. He peeked in and announced, "I found him!"

"Found who?" asked Juan.

"Found you. You're missing again," said Drew.

"Nope, I'm right here, checking out this bag of cow food. If Farmer Fandangle's cows give *out* organic milk, then they must take *in* . . ."

"One hundred percent organic feed! Good observation, sonny," said Farmer Fandangle as the rest of the class joined them. "Remember, ya are what ya eat."

"Let's get going. There's lots more to see," said Mrs. Shepherd as they followed Farmer Fandangle to the henhouse.

The Henhouse

There were *bawks* and *squawks* everywhere!

More surprising were the *whooshes* and *whirs* of the conveyor belts that transported the eggs from the hens' nests to waiting cartons.

"Egg gathering sure has changed over the years," Mrs. Shepherd said.

"Yup," agreed Farmer Fandangle. "Changed in a good way. Come on, time to check out the sheep."

"Just a minute," said Mrs. Shepherd. "Before we go, time . . ."

"For a head count," finished the chaperones. "We counted four sets of five and had two extra students, so that makes . . ."

"Twenty-two!" shouted the students.

"Good math," said Mrs. Shepherd, "but wrong number. We're missing someone again. Hurry, everyone, let's find him."

Josephina felt a rush of air through a crack in the wall and went to check it out. "I found him!" she yelled against the wind.

"Found who?" asked Juan, gazing up at the wind turbines.

"Found you. You're missing again."

"Nope, I'm right here. When I saw all those henhouse contraptions, I wondered where they got their power from."

"Good thinkin', sonny," said Farmer Fandangle. "I almost forgot about showin' these to everyone." He patted Juan on the back as he explained how wind power supplied the energy to run his farm.

"Now let's go check out them there sheep."

There were *bleats* and *blats* everywhere!
The sheep got into line. Farmer Fandangle then showed how easy it was to shave off their wool.

Mrs. Shepherd said, "Sheep shearing sure has changed over the years."

"That's right," agreed Farmer Fandangle. "Changed in a good way. Follow me, everyone. I've got one more special thing to show all of ya."

"Just a minute," said Mrs. Shepherd. "Before we go . . ."

"Time for a head count," finished the chaperones. "We counted seven sets of three and had one extra student, so that makes . . ."

"Twenty-two!" shouted the students.

"Good math," said Mrs. Shepherd, "but wrong number. We're missing you-know-who. Come on, everyone, get looking."

Ima spied a familiar face over at the farm-house. "Guess who I found?" she yelled.

"Juan Dore-Nomad!" everyone answered when they caught up.

Juan said, "I wasn't lost. I just wondered what happened to the wool after it was sheared."

Farmer Fandangle grinned.

Then he explained how he used natural dyes to color his wool—spinach leaves to make green, acorns to make brown, and dandelion flowers to make yellow.

Beep-beep!

"The bus is here. Time to go back to school," said Mrs. Shepherd.

Toot-toot!

"My ride is here, too," said Farmer Fandangle.

"Are you going back to school with us?" asked Juan.

"No, sonny. This is a ride for two special little ones I wanted to show ya."

Farmer Fandangle headed into the barn and then came out looking upset. "By golly, they're gone."

"Who's gone?" asked Mrs. Shepherd.

"The calves, the two calves I was donatin' to charity. I got them ready to go before you came this mornin', but now they're missin'."

"Two lost calves. Get looking, everyone," said Mrs. Shepherd.

The students skittered and scattered in every direction—the barn, the henhouse, the hill with the turbines, the sheep shed . . .

The chaperones flung their clipboards in frustration as they tried to count all those scurrying kids.

Until someone yelled,

"I FOUND THEM!"

It was Juan Dore-Nomad, peeking his head out the front door of the farmhouse.

Everyone hurried inside, and there were the calves cuddled up together on Farmer Fandangle's bed.

"How'd ya know to look here, sonny?"

"Well, I just thought about where I'd wander off to if I was leaving home for the first time," said Juan. "Someplace cozy."

Farmer Fandangle slapped his knee and said, "By gorry, good thinkin', sonny!"

The kids were sorry to see the calves go, until Farmer Fandangle explained that they were going to help a family start a new farm. As the calves walked into their carrier, Mrs. Shepherd's class reluctantly climbed onto their bus.

"Do we have to leave so soon?" asked Maybella.
"Come again. You're always welcome," said Farmer Fandangle. "Especially you, sonny," he said to Juan. "I like the way you think!"

" . . .twenty, twenty-one, twenty-two . . ." said the chaperones as they counted the students one last time.

"Uh-oh," said the chaperones.

"Not again!" cried the kids.

"You know what to do," said Mrs. Shepherd as everyone began checking under and over their seats.

"Twenty-three!" shouted Juan, who popped up with a big grin.

"Good math," said Mrs. Shepherd, "and the *right* number! Let's get going before it changes again."